CREEP OUT

CEMETERIES

VALERIE BODDEN

CREATIVE EDUCATION

Published by Creative Education
P.O. Box 227, Mankato, Minnesota 56002
Creative Education is an imprint of The Creative Company
www.thecreativecompany.us

Design and production by Chelsey Luther
Art direction by Rita Marshall
Printed in China

Photographs by Alamy (Guy Corbishley, Zoonar GmbH), Dreamstime (Fernbach Antal, Sandra Cunningham, Flynt, Javarman, Koya79, Missjelena, Zacarias Pereira Da Mata, Perseomedusa, Matthew Ragen, Anatoly Repin, Elena Schweitzer, Vickifrance, Welburnstuart), Getty Images (PATRICK KOVARIK), Shutterstock (Colin D. Young)

Library of Congress Cataloging-in-Publication Data
Names: Bodden, Valerie, author.
Title: Cemeteries / Valerie Bodden.
Series: Creep out.
Includes bibliographical references and index.
Summary: Feel goosebumps begin to form as this title explores cemeteries around the world, surveying common cemetery features and creepy stories about these places.

Identifiers: LCCN 2016033587 / ISBN 978-1-60818-806-2 (hardcover) / ISBN 978-1-56660-854-1 (eBook)
Subjects: LCSH: 1. Haunted cemeteries—Juvenile literature. 2. Cemeteries—Psychological aspects—Juvenile literature. 3. Parapsychology—Juvenile literature.
Classification: LCC BF1474.3.B63 2017 / DDC 133.1/22—dc23

CCSS: RI.1.1, 2, 3, 4, 5, 6, 10; RI.2.1, 2, 3, 4, 5, 6, 7, 10; RI.3.1, 2, 3, 4, 5, 10; RF.1.1, 3, 4; RF.2.3, 4; RF.3.3, 4

First Edition HC 9 8 7 6 5 4 3 2 1

Table *of* Contents

Introduction

A gate slams shut behind you. Tombstones stand around you. A cool breeze slides over your skin. You shiver. You are in a cemetery.

FOR HUNDREDS OF YEARS, CHURCHES WERE IN CHARGE OF BURYING PEOPLE, SO CEMETERIES WERE OFTEN NEARBY.

Burial Places

Cemeteries are places where dead bodies are buried. People have buried the dead for thousands of years. Cemeteries were the first public parks. They gave people a place to walk and visit. Today, people go to cemeteries to remember their loved ones.

IN CROWDED CITIES, SOMETIMES THERE IS NOT MUCH GREEN SPACE IN A CEMETERY, BUT PEOPLE LEAVE PLANTS THERE.

SOME CEMETERIES ARE SO OLD THAT THE HEAVY TOMBSTONES HAVE STARTED TO SINK INTO THE GROUND.

TOMBSTONES mark the graves in a cemetery. Most tombstones are made of rock. Many cemeteries are fenced in. Trees might grow in the cemetery.

What Makes Cemeteries Creepy?

CEMETERIES creep some people out. Thick weeds grow in old cemeteries. Moss covers run-down tombstones. Huge statues tower overhead. They look like people or angels. Some people think there are ghosts in cemeteries. Other people worry about vampires.

STONES SUCH AS ALABASTER, LIMESTONE, AND MARBLE ARE COMMONLY USED TO MAKE STATUES.

Famous Cemeteries

CEMETERIES can be found around the world. The city of New Orleans is in Louisiana. It has 42 cemeteries. The bodies are buried in above-ground tombs. These look like small buildings.

THE NEW ORLEANS CEMETERIES ARE KNOWN AS "CITIES OF THE DEAD," WITH THEIR HOUSE-LIKE TOMBS AND PATHS.

MANY PARTS OF HIGHGATE GOT OVERGROWN UNTIL PEOPLE STARTED RESTORING THE CEMETERY IN THE 1970s.

HIGHGATE Cemetery is in London, England. It is more than 150 years old. Its statues and tombstones are crumbling. Trees and vines grow everywhere. Some people think a vampire haunts the cemetery.

THE Paris Catacombs (*CAT-uh-komz*) are in France. They are tunnels below the city. More than 6 million people are buried there. Bones are stacked along the tunnel walls. Some form shapes such as hearts or crosses.

A TOUR OF THE CATACOMBS TAKES ABOUT 45 MINUTES TO COVER THE 1.2 MILES (2 KM) OF TUNNELS.

Creep Out!

CEMETERIES do not look scary during the day. But at night, the moon shines on tombstones. The wind moans through trees. Will you get creeped out?

MOONLIGHT AND SHADOWS CAN SOMETIMES MAKE YOU SEE THINGS THAT ARE NOT REALLY THERE.

Diagram *of a* Cemetery

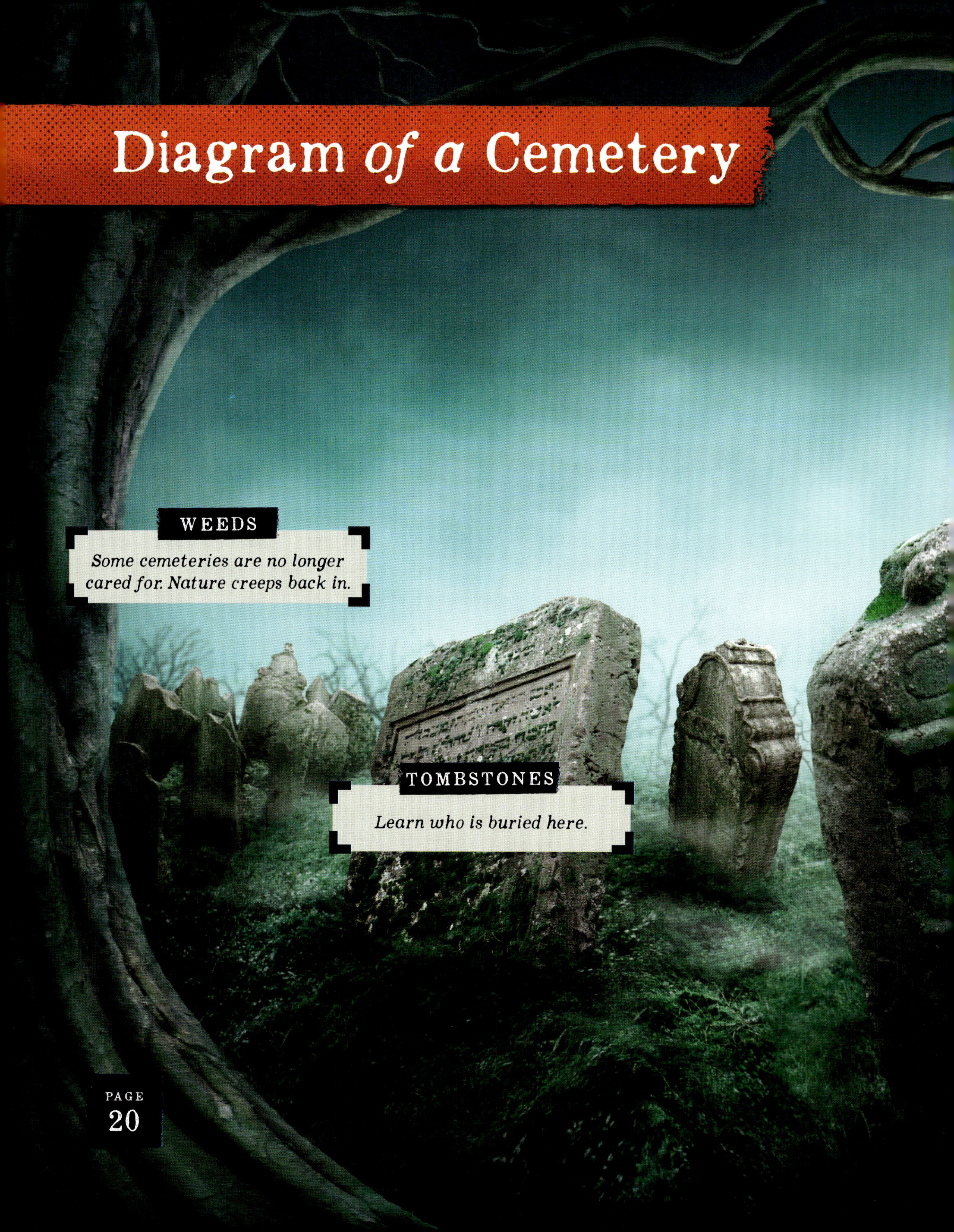

GRAVES

Bodies are in caskets under your feet.

STATUES

Are their eyes following you?

PATHS

Be careful not to get lost.

ENTRANCE

A gate blocks some cemeteries. Enter if you dare.

Glossary

GRAVES—holes in the ground where bodies are buried

MOSS—low, leafy plants that grow in patches on rocks, trees, or soil

TOMBSTONES—stones with words carved in them to mark a grave

VAMPIRES—bodies of dead people that are said to come out of their graves at night to suck people's blood

Read More

Ferut, Michael. *St. Louis Cemetery No. 1.* Minneapolis: Bellwether Media, 2015.

Von Finn, Denny. *Paris Catacombs.* Minneapolis: Bellwether Media, 2014.

Websites

Kids.net: List of Famous Cemeteries

http://encyclopedia.kids.net.au/page/li/List__of__famous__cemeteries
Check out this list of famous cemeteries around the world.

YouTube: Explore Highgate Cemetery

https://www.youtube.com/watch?v=Xc__FvntP2v0
Watch a video of pictures from this creepy cemetery.

⚠ Note: Every effort has been made to ensure that any websites listed above were active at the time of publication and suitable for children. However, because of the nature of the Internet, it is impossible to guarantee that these sites will remain active indefinitely or that their contents will not be altered.

Index